little Miss Busy

by Roger Hargreaves

PSS!
PRICE STERN SLOAN

Little Miss Busy loved nothing more than to be hard at work keeping herself busy.

As busy as a bee.

In fact, as busy as a hive of bees.

Every day she would get up at three o'clock in the morning.

Then Little Miss Busy would read a chapter from her favorite book.

The book was called *Work Is Good for You*.

And then she would get down to the housework.

She would begin by tidying up,
and then sweeping,
and dusting,
and scrubbing,
and polishing,
until everything was spotless.

She would clean her house from top to bottom and
then from bottom to top, just to make sure.

She even dusted the bread and polished the butter.

She wasn't happy unless she was busy working.

She didn't rest all day long—not for a minute. Not even for a second.

From three o'clock in the morning until after midnight.

Until last Monday, that is.

Little Miss Busy wasn't up at three o'clock.

She wasn't up by six o'clock.

She wasn't even out of bed by nine o'clock.

She was sick.

"I won't be able to do any work!" she cried.
"Oh, calamity!"

She phoned Doctor Make-you-well.

Five minutes later he was standing at the side of her bed.

He asked her to stick out her tongue.

He examined her throat.

And he looked at her hands and feet.

"What you need is rest, a lot of rest," he said with a big smile.

"A lot of rest," repeated Little Miss Busy to herself. "Oh, calamity!"

There was a loud THUMP!

Which was the sound of Little Miss Busy
falling over backward,
onto the bed,
luckily for her.

On Tuesday, Mr. Strong came to see Little Miss Busy.

He brought her 72 eggs.

That's a lot of eggs!

"There is nothing like eggs for giving you strength," said Mr. Strong.

After eating the seventy-second egg Little Miss Busy was feeling much better.

That was, until Mr. Strong said, "Now you must rest to get your strength up."

There was a loud THUMP!

Which was the sound of Little Miss Busy
falling over backward,
onto the bed,
luckily for her.

On Wednesday, Mr. Greedy came to visit.

He brought an enormous bowl of food.

"I always find that eating a big meal makes me feel better," said Mr. Greedy.

Little Miss Busy ate all of it.

She felt better than ever.

That was, until Mr. Greedy said, "Now you must rest to calm your stomach."

There was a loud THUMP!

And you know what that was, don't you?

That's right!

Little Miss Busy had fallen over backward.

On Thursday, Mr. Nonsense dropped by to see Little Miss Busy.

He brought her . . . an umbrella!

"Hello," he said. "I hear you're feeling well. You don't need to rest. . . ."

Little Miss Busy jumped for joy, right out of bed. "You need a vacation!" finished Mr. Nonsense.

There was a loud THUMP!
That's right. Little Miss Busy had fallen over backward . . . again.

"There, you look better already," said Mr. Nonsense, and left . . .

. . . out the open window.

Little Miss Busy picked herself up.

A small smile formed on her face.

Something Mr. Nonsense had said had actually made sense.

She had never thought of going on vacation before.

The more she thought about it the happier she felt.

She thought of all the fun things she could do:

There was the planning and organizing,
there was all the shopping she would have to do,
there was the packing,
and she would have to learn the language,
and read lots of books about the place she was
going to visit.

That's a lot of work!

Little Miss Busy smiled happily.

The following Thursday, she was awake at three o'clock in the morning.

Everything was ready.

Little Miss Busy had had one of the busiest weeks of her life.

Which is saying something!

She had only one thing left to do.

And that was . . .

. . . to learn how to relax!